Welcome to the world of Beast Quest!

Tom was once an ordinary village boy, until he travelled to the City, met King Hugo and discovered his destiny. Now he is the Master of the Beasts, sworn to defend Avantia and its people against Evil. Tom draws on the might of the magical Golden Armour, and is protected by powerful tokens granted to him by the Good Beasts of Avantia. Together with his loyal companion Elenna, Tom is always ready to visit new lands and tackle the enemies of the realm.

While there's blood in his veins, Tom will never give up the Quest...

GARGANTUA
THE SILENT ASSASSIN

BY ADAM BLADE

ORCHARD

With special thanks to Tabitha Jones

www.beastquest.co.uk

ORCHARD BOOKS

First published in Great Britain in 2022 by The Watts Publishing Group

1 3 5 7 9 10 8 6 4 2

Text © Beast Quest Limited 2022
Cover and inside illustrations by Steve Sims
© Beast Quest Limited 2022

Beast Quest is a registered trademark of Beast Quest Limited
Series created by Beast Quest Limited, London

A CIP catalogue record for this book is available from the British Library.

ISBN 978 1 40836 534 2

Printed in Great Britain

The paper and board used in this book are made from wood from responsible sources

Orchard Books
An imprint of Hachette Children's Group
Part of The Watts Publishing Group Limited
Carmelite House, 50 Victoria Embankment, London EC4Y 0DZ

An Hachette UK Company
www.hachette.co.uk
www.hachettechildrens.co.uk

There are special gold coins to collect in this book. You will earn one coin for every chapter you read.

Find out what to do with your coins at the end of the book.

CONTENTS

For a time, I was the most powerful Master of the Beasts who ever walked this land. A royal prince. A courageous hero. People chanted my name.

But at the peak of my fame, it was taken from me by cowards.

For almost three centuries my spirit has wandered the realms. In ghostly form, I have searched for the one magical token that will bring me back.

And now I have found it, Avantia will pay for her treachery.

Only a fool would stand in my path.

Karadin

THE SERPENT OF STONEWIN

"What a mess!" Elenna said as she and Tom made their way through the dim, deserted streets of Millden towards the village stables. "I wish we could help the villagers rebuild."

Tom squinted through the gloom, running his eyes over the destruction left by their battle with

Raptex. Broken windows, smashed
by the griffin-Beast's deafening
cry, stared darkly back at him from
either side of the street. Some of
the buildings were little more than
empty husks with splintered timbers
poking through holes in their roofs
and walls.

Tom shook his head at the
devastation. "We'll ask King Hugo
to send aid when we get back to the
palace," he said.

He and Elenna were on a Quest
to prevent the Evil ghost-prince
Karadin from stealing Avantia's
throne. Karadin had once been
Master of the Beasts, and since
rising from the grave he had

already awakened three terrible creatures. Tom and Elenna had defeated each one in turn, but Karadin had absorbed the Beasts' magical essences and was now stronger than ever, while Tom's own powers were failing fast.

Glancing up, he noticed the first grey streaks of dawn light were already creeping into the sky. His stomach clenched with dread. "We'd better hurry!" he said.

As they reached the stables, Tom shouldered the door open and he and Elenna pushed through into the warmth inside. Tom's stallion Storm tossed his head, whinnying softly; Silver, Elenna's wolf, yawned and got stiffly to his feet.

"I know," Elenna said gently, running a hand through his thick coat. "It's far too early!"

While Tom saddled Storm, Elenna packed away the bread and fruit they had been given by the villagers. As he tightened the final buckle, Tom heard the soft clearing of a throat. He turned and made out the faint, shimmering outline of Karadin's younger brother, Prince Loris. The ghost was tall and broad, with the bearing of a man still in his youth. Tom felt a surge of pity. Loris had guided them on their Quest so far, but, like Tom, his strength was waning as Karadin's grew. Now only his sorrowful eyes were clearly visible.

"Loris," Tom said, bowing his head in greeting. "Do you know where Karadin is heading next?"

"My brother will make his way to Stonewin Volcano," Loris said. His voice was barely more than a sigh, and Tom had to lean in close to hear him. "Karadin will do all in his power to awaken the terrible Beast who lies there."

"That's Epos's home," Elenna said.

Loris nodded. "But Epos is not the only Beast of Stonewin. Long ago, my brother and I travelled there to face the mighty serpent Gargantua. We became separated…" A grimace of pain flitted across Loris's pale, translucent features. "It was my final battle. Watch…"

Loris spread his hands as if opening a book. At the same moment, Tom's vision blurred, and the stable floor seemed to drop away beneath his feet. He staggered, trying to find his balance as a sudden glare of bright sunlight blinded him. Focussing his eyes, Tom found himself standing on a high mountain ledge, staring into the mouth of a cave. A strong wind swirled around him, and from deep inside the cave ahead he could hear the muffled clashes and bangs of a battle, along with the furious hiss of a Beast.

Tom tried to lunge towards the cave, to add his strength to the fight, but he couldn't move. His body wasn't his own. Just then the loudest hiss yet echoed from the darkness, followed by a man's anguished cry, cut short...

Loris spoke into the sudden quiet. "I feared my brother was dead," he said. "I was wrong."

In the vision, Karadin burst from

the cave. His cloak was torn, and he held a bloodied sword aloft, but he appeared unhurt – and young. The prince's eyes were a clear, bright blue instead of the black holes of the ghost-prince Tom had met on this Quest. Something on Karadin's finger

caught the light of the sun – something Tom recognised: a silver ring in the shape of a snake eating its own tail. It bore a single clear stone that shone like a star.

"I had never seen the ring before that day," Loris said. "I should have known what it meant…"

Tom saw the awful moment unfold: as Loris turned, Karadin lunged, thrusting his sword deep into his brother's mortal flesh.

Beside Tom, Elenna gasped in horror, and the vision dissolved into ripples of colour like driving rain on a pane of glass. When Tom could see again, he was standing in the dim stable once more. Silence briefly fell as the shock of the murder sank in.

"I had always known Karadin was ambitious," Loris said. "But I never thought he would stoop that low. I can only believe that Gargantua somehow corrupted the goodness in him."

Fury burned inside Tom. "While there is blood in my veins, I will avenge your death," he promised. "Tell me, where in Stonewin does Gargantua lie?"

"There is a caldera on the eastern side of the volcano, which Gargantua has made her lair. It was covered long ago by rock falls and lava flows, but the serpent's remains lie deep inside the mountain. I have to warn you, though: if Karadin and the serpent Gargantua are ever bound together again, my brother will become unstoppable. And I..." Loris sighed, his faint outline wavering. "I shall be no more."

"I won't let that happen," Tom vowed, but as he spoke, wind gusted through the stable door, and what was left of Loris's translucent form frayed into swirling tatters of mist and vanished...

1

FRIEND TURNED FOE

The day passed in a blur of speed and rolling grassland as Storm carried Tom and Elenna east over the Central Plains. Refreshed by his night's rest, Silver kept pace at the stallion's side, his grey fur rippling in the wind as he ran. By mid-afternoon, the rugged heights of Stonewin

Volcano loomed above them.

Tom pulled Storm to a halt beside a stream and swung himself from the saddle. Elenna slid to the ground too, stooping to ruffle Silver's fur gently. As Storm drank, Tom ran a hand over his horse's dark, glossy coat. He noticed a few new strands of white hair amongst the black. *How long have they been there?* Tom realised with a pang that he might not be able to rely on his stallion for much longer… He banished the thought from his mind.

"Thank you," Tom told his horse. "Now rest with Silver. We'll be as quick as we can."

After filling Storm's nosebag with

oats and topping up their water flasks, Tom and Elenna made their way towards the base of the volcano. It towered above them, a few grey puffs of smoke billowing from a wide crater at its summit and another smaller crater, lower down and to the east. There was no sign of Karadin, nor any Beast.

"Let's get this over with," Elenna said, and together she and Tom began to climb.

The ground around Stonewin was rich and fertile, but the volcano itself was barren, without so much as a blade of grass. They walked over dark rock made from hardened lava flows contorted into ripples and folds, which reflected the heat of the sun, thinning the air. With no breeze or shade to relieve the heat, Tom was soon sweaty and parched. Though he and Elenna pushed themselves onward as fast as they could, frustration and worry gnawed at him. He knew that at any moment, Karadin could realise his Evil goal and awaken Gargantua. Then all would be lost.

As Tom and Elenna climbed higher, the terrain grew more treacherous still. They had to skirt around great slabs of stone that jutted from the mountainside at odd angles, and scramble over piles of rubble. Sheer ravines cut across their path, so deep Tom couldn't see the bottom.

Elenna dropped a pebble into one, and they both listened...

Nothing.

Finally Tom heard a faint clatter, quickly followed by a deep, resounding *boom*. The mountain gave a terrific shudder.

Elenna winced. "Remind me not to do that again!" she said.

They scrambled onward in silence, making slow and steady progress towards the eastern crater. Tom kept an eye out for Karadin, but the only other living creatures around seemed to be the vultures circling endlessly above.

Eventually, Tom stopped on a narrow plateau and ran his eyes up the short stretch of mountainside left to climb. All he could see was stark, empty rock and a pile of fallen rubble from a recent avalanche. He called on the magical eyesight of his golden helmet. At once, the heights swam into focus, a magnified view of the same lifeless stone.

"Where is he?" Tom growled.

"Maybe he's already reached the caldera," Elenna said nervously.

"Quite possibly," said Tom. "I should warn Epos. Maybe she can keep Karadin busy until we catch up." Tom put his hand to the red jewel in his belt and called to the Beast with his mind.

Epos, I need your help!

The jewel gave off a faint warmth, and Tom felt a tingle of emotion in the back of his mind – something between confusion and fear.

Epos, he repeated, *is all well?*

Again, Tom sensed a flicker of bewildered alarm from the phoenix, but she didn't reply.

Tom balled his fists. "I can't reach her," he told Elenna. "And Karadin could be awakening Gargantua as we speak!"

"We're not far from the summit," Elenna said. "And if Karadin had already found the snake-Beast, I'm sure there would be some sign. There is still hope."

Together they scrambled on as

fast as they could, clambering up
the steep, craggy rise, loose scree
tumbling down behind them.

Suddenly, an ear-splitting shriek
rent the air. Nerves jangling, Tom
looked up just in time to see a
familiar tawny form emerge from
behind an outcrop of rock.

Epos!

As the mighty flame bird rose,
her broad wingspan momentarily
eclipsed the sun. Then Tom saw
something that made him clench his
jaw in fury: Karadin, sitting astride
the phoenix's back, a triumphant
grin on his face.

The ghost-prince pointed down at
the fallen rubble on the mountainside

above Tom and Elenna. In response, Epos drew back her taloned foot and hurled a blazing ball of flame towards

it. The fiery orb slammed into the mountainside with a *boom*! Huge chunks of stone exploded outwards.

Tom dived behind a jutting slab of rock, tugging Elenna with him.

"Now I know why Epos was silent," Tom said. "Karadin has enchanted her. But what are they doing?" Another *boom* rang out above, the whole mountain quaking as more broken fragments of rock tumbled around them.

"Blasting a path through to Gargantua, by the sound of it," Elenna said, wiping a bleeding cut on her cheek where a stone had struck her.

Tom put his hand to the red jewel in his belt. *Epos, stop!* he told Epos with his mind. *You don't have to obey Karadin!*

A wave of emotion slammed into Tom, so strong it made him gasp. Anger, fear, confusion, pain... His head felt as if it might burst with the force of Epos's anguish. *I...can't disobey...the Master of the Beasts...*

I *am your Master*, Tom said. *I command you to stop!*

Another surge of torment hit him, blinding him with agony and throwing him to his knees. Tom clutched his throbbing head. *Must obey...* Epos's voice was shrill and panicked, a hot knife driving through Tom's skull. *Beware... Gargantua shall rise. She... will destroy...everything!*

Elenna helped Tom to his feet. "What is it?" she asked, her brow creased with worry.

"Karadin has grown too strong," Tom said. "Epos can't resist him!"

Peering out from their hiding place, Tom saw the phoenix hovering above the crater she had blasted.

Sitting tall on her back, his eyes blazing with exultation, Karadin pointed down at the hole once more.

The Good Beast sent a sizzling jet of flames towards it, burning away more rock, making it glow red hot.

Tom drew his sword. "We have to stop Epos," he told Elenna. "But…be careful. I don't want to hurt her!"

Elenna fitted an arrow to her bow and took aim, then shook her head. "I can't get a clear shot at Karadin!"

Tom could feel the heat from Epos's flames even from their hiding place. At any moment, she would break through the rock… He leapt out into the open, gasping as a wall of hot air hit him. Tom lifted his shield and, calling on Ferno's dragon scale to deflect the heat, half-ran, half-staggered up the slope towards Epos. But Karadin turned, his black eyes narrowing.

"Stop them!" Karadin shrieked, tugging at Epos's feathers. The flame bird's head whipped around. She flapped her wings, hovering for an instant, then dived, sending a roaring jet of fire towards Tom.

The flames hit the wood of Tom's shield and curled around its edges, scalding his throat, making it impossible to breathe. The onslaught seemed to go on and on, searing Tom's skin and singeing his hair. Then it stopped. Panting and dizzy, Tom fell back to shelter behind the rock.

"What now?" Elenna asked. At that moment, a huge shadow passed over them. Dread stirring in his gut, Tom peered out from their hiding place to see Epos land at the edge of the

crater. Karadin vaulted down from the phoenix's back and gestured to the great hole in the rock.

"Dive!" Karadin commanded. "Break

through into the volcano!"

Even without reaching for his red jewel, Tom could feel Epos's fear and horror. But despite her anguish, the flame bird flapped her wings and rose high into the sky above the volcano.

"NO!" Tom shouted. *You will be hurt*, he told Epos. *You must not do as Karadin says!*

I cannot disobey… Epos replied. She threw her wings back and plummeted.

Tom held his breath as the Good Beast hurtled towards the mountainside. Elenna had her arrow trained on Epos's breast, but she didn't fire. They both stood paralysed, powerless to stop what was about to happen.

INTO THE FIRE

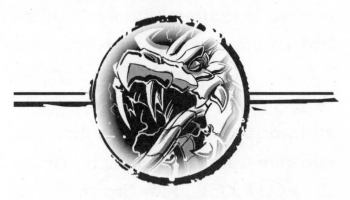

Tom's heart gave a painful leap as
Epos slammed into the volcano,
beak-first. The mountain shook, a
billowing cloud of smoke erupting
upwards. Tom tugged Elenna close
and lifted his shield above their heads
as a hail of rocks pelted down. As soon
as the storm of falling rubble was
over, Tom and Elenna raced towards

Epos. She lay just inside the opening she had created in the volcano, half covered in shattered stone. Karadin had already vanished into darkness.

Tom placed a hand on the dusty feathers of Epos's neck. They were still warm, but the phoenix didn't stir. Tom waited, watching to see the rise and fall of the breath in her chest... Then, to his relief, she opened her eyes groggily. But Tom could see she was badly injured: one of her wings was folded back at a hideous angle, and her beak was cracked and bleeding. Together, Tom and Elenna carefully cleared the worst of the rubble from Epos's body. Then Tom took the healing

talon from
his shield.
Epos had
given the
token to him
on one of
his earliest
Quests. He
had never
thought she
would need
its help herself.

"Lie still," Tom told her. "You
will be better soon." While Elenna
brushed the rock dust from Epos's
body, Tom rested the talon against
one of the crooked flight feathers in
her broken wing. Slowly, painfully

slowly, the feather unfolded, regaining its sleek, glossy shape. But there were so many feathers to heal!

Master... Epos's voice was weak, but calm. *I am sorry I fought you. The other Master...he is too strong. Do not waste time healing me. I am old and my wounds too great. Go after Karadin while there is still time!*

Tom could hardly speak for the lump in his throat. "I can't leave you like this," he said hoarsely.

You must, Epos replied. *I know this Beast. She has long tormented me, invading my dreams. If Gargantua rises...if Karadin commands the mighty iron serpent,*

Avantia is lost.

Tom's heart ached at the idea of leaving Epos. But he knew she was right. He thrust the healing talon into Elenna's hand. "Heal her," he said. "Then come after me if you can."

Elenna looked from Tom to Epos, then back again, her eyes clouded with worry. Finally, she nodded. "Take a torch from my pack," she said.

Casting one last, sorrowful look back at Epos, Tom scooped up the torch and set off.

Deep inside the hole that the flame bird had blasted, Tom found the narrow opening of a tunnel. He lit the torch and ducked inside. The rotten-egg stink of brimstone hung heavy in the stale, dead air, along with a muggy heat that seemed to come from the rock itself. Tom covered his face with his sleeve, but still, the stench was almost suffocating. What little daylight there was quickly faded behind him, and though the torch burned brightly, its light barely seemed to stretch more than a few paces ahead. As Tom followed the tunnel deeper into the heart of the volcano, the rock floor trembled beneath his feet; ominous groans and rumbles echoed from the darkness. The walls and ceiling seemed to press in on him, and despite the heat, a cold sweat broke out on his skin.

The way got steadily narrower until there was barely space for Tom to pass. He turned sideways and sucked in his chest, making himself as small as he could. The walls pressed against him, squeezing his ribs so that he could hardly draw breath. Every instinct urged him to turn back. *But Karadin went this way…* he told himself. *It must be wide enough.* Suddenly his boot jammed in a crack as he tried to squeeze through. Panic flared in his chest, and he wrenched at his foot, trying to get free. It was no use. *I'm stuck!* Tom forced himself to breathe slowly, to not panic…and somehow, managed to wriggle his way free.

He edged onward, grazing his knees and elbows on the rough stone, just holding his panic in check, until finally the crack widened. Tom wiped the sweat from his face, took a long shaky breath and kept going.

As he hurried on, his footsteps strangely muffled in the stifling darkness, he thought he heard another noise – a soft hiss of breath. The sound came again, clearer than ever, but Tom couldn't place it. It seemed to come from every direction at once…or from inside his head. Soft and venomous, it made his skin prickle with dread. *Come...* The rasping hiss grew stronger, whispering in Tom's mind, and now he recognised it as the unmistakable sound of a serpent-Beast.

Gargantua!

Come to me, Masssster, the snake hissed. *Come and I shall rise...*

She's calling to Karadin, Tom realised. *That means I'm not too late!* He drew his sword and quickened his step. The passage twisted and turned, always heading downward, and Gargantua's voice went on and on. It was a vile whisper in Tom's mind that seemed to slither up and down his spine, setting his nerves on edge.

Come… The voice grew stronger, filling Tom's head, rushing and whooshing like the sea… Like smoke coiling into the sky… Like sleep, rolling over him in dizzying waves. Becoming suddenly aware of his muddled thoughts, Tom stopped and shook his head. But he couldn't shift the groggy feeling.

It must be the fumes, he thought as he continued further down the passage, deep into the heart of the mountain. Rounding a sharp corner, he spotted the sullen glow of deep red light ahead. *Lava?* The heat and stench of rotten eggs grew stronger, making Tom's head swim. Each time his thoughts began to roam, drifting away with Gargantua's soft voice, he pinched himself hard, but he felt as if he was walking in a dream. *Or a nightmare.* Cold, clammy sweat stuck his tunic to his back. His mouth was so dry he could barely swallow. And, like a nightmare that he couldn't wake from, Gargantua's voice went on and on. *Come... come...Master of the Beasts...*

With the red light all around him now, Tom no longer needed his torch. He turned a final corner and pulled up short. The tunnel opened into an immense high-ceilinged cavern. The chamber floor was criss-crossed with sluggish streams of flowing

lava that bubbled and boiled,
spitting out globs of molten rock.
In the centre of the chamber lay the
vast shape of an iron cobra, coiled
as if ready to strike – and before this
monstrosity stood Karadin. No part

of the Evil prince was transparent now. His whole body looked solid and muscular, and as Tom watched, he rested a hand on Gargantua's massive head, the ring on his finger glowing with a searing white light.

Tom felt suddenly hollow with dread. *I'm too late…Karadin is raising the Beast!*

1

THE POWER OF THE RING

Tom scanned the chamber floor, looking for a path through the deadly lava, but he could see he was already too late. The ring on Karadin's finger crackled with strands of platinum light. The magical energy coiled up the ghost-prince's arm and swirled around

Gargantua's body, fizzing like bolts of lightning. Where the blazing streams of energy touched Karadin his flesh scaled over, turning hard and grey – already his forearm and hand looked like solid iron. And at Karadin's side, Gargantua stirred. One eye opened, showing a crack of bright blue light.

I must stop this! Raising his sword, Tom called on the magic of his golden boots and leapt. Flying over streams of molten lava, he kicked out hard with both legs… *Boof!* His feet slammed into the small of Karadin's back.

With a cry of surprise, Karadin fell forward, crashing into Gargantua's glowing metal body. Tom landed less than a hand-span from a bubbling lava stream. The stench of it caught in his throat, stinging his eyes, but he lifted his sword, ready to fight. Karadin spun around, his teeth bared with hatred and his metal fist drawn back.

"I admire your persistence, boy," he spat. "But my patience is wearing thin. You have no right to be here. In fact, you shouldn't even exist. *I* am the Master of the Beasts and the kingdom only needs one!" As Karadin swung his fist, Tom blocked with his sword. The sound of metal on metal rang like a gong being struck, and the force of the blow ricocheted up Tom's

arm. It was accompanied by a sharp jolt of energy that fizzed though his hand and fingers, loosening his grip on his sword.

He almost dropped his weapon but managed to tighten his grip just in time.

What was that?!

"You will not leave here alive," Karadin shouted. "I alone shall be Master of the Beasts and I will be your king too!"

"You are no Master!" Tom cried. "No true Master would murder his own brother in cold blood!"

Karadin's eyes bulged, and his face darkened as he let out an incoherent screech of rage. He swung his fist again. Tom lifted his shield, deflecting the blow, but once again, a powerful fizz of energy seared through him, weakening his limbs and throwing him back towards a lava flow... He just managed to catch his balance as he reached the edge, the heel of his boot smoking as it touched the molten rock.

A loud, venomous hiss echoed through the chamber. Tom glanced towards Gargantua to see she now had both eyes open. Her forked tongue flickered from between her needle-sharp fangs, and she hissed again: a long, chilly sound, horribly like laughter.

"You are too late," Karadin said, his eyes flashing with glee. "Gargantua will rise and I will be king and Master of the Beasts!"

"Never!" Tom cried, slashing for Karadin's throat. Almost effortlessly, the Evil prince lifted his iron hand and batted Tom's blade aside with a deafening *CLANG*! Tom felt another shock of pain fizzing up his arm, deadening it. Tom tried to lift his sword, but his limb wouldn't obey him. Karadin lunged, and Tom scrambled back away from the Evil ghost, quickly passing his sword to his left hand, adjusting his grip. Gargantua's vile hiss echoed across the cavern, followed by the slithering scrape of metal scales on rock. Glancing towards the Beast, Tom saw her sinuous body uncoiling...and from the corner of his eye, he registered Karadin's hand shooting towards him. Tom ducked, but Karadin was too fast...

Tom's vision blurred as the Evil prince grabbed him by the throat and lifted him off his feet. Where Karadin's metal hand touched Tom, searing shocks of energy knifed through him, turning his body to jelly. Hanging in Karadin's grip, unable to breathe, Tom kicked and twisted, trying to get free, but he was too weak.

"Die!" Karadin spat, his lips twisting in an evil sneer as he hurled Tom across the cavern. Tom hit the far wall, his body sinking to the ground as limply as a pile of rags. He tried to stand but his legs felt rubbery, and he couldn't move. Karadin was on him in an instant.

"You have failed! I am the true Master of the Beasts, and I take my birthright now!" Karadin roared, drawing his fist back to strike the final killing blow.

I will not die this way! Tom vowed. He couldn't stand…he could barely move – but he would not give in to Evil. As Karadin's fist hurtled towards Tom, he gathered all his meagre strength, gripped his sword with both hands and sent it flashing through the air. The blade sliced cleanly through Karadin's arm, chopping it off it at the elbow. His iron hand

hit the floor with a dull *clang*.

Karadin gaped at his severed stump, where the flesh was shrivelling and darkening... Then his eyes widened in shock, and he looked down at his feet. Tom stared in horror too. Karadin's legs had blackened just as his stump had, like mummified remains. They started to crumble, turning to dust as if being eaten away by centuries of decay all at once... Karadin's legs were next, rapidly disintegrating into dry grey powder that fell to the ground like sand through a timer. His torso followed, caving in on itself, slumping to the cavern floor. And last of all, his face dissolved,

complete
with its
puzzled
frown. Now
there was
nothing
left of the
prince but a
pile of dust
and a single

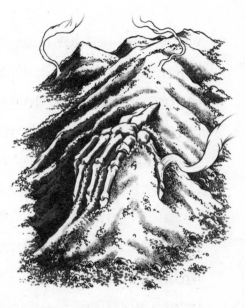

skeletal hand. Tom blinked as if
waking from a bad dream. It had
happened so fast! But Karadin was
gone.

Finally able to move, Tom
staggered to his feet. Then a rasping
hiss echoed all around him, making
him turn. *Massster!* The Beast's

voice was louder than ever – so loud it seemed to fill Tom's mind, leaving no room for any other thought. *The ring!* Gargantua hissed.

Looking down, Tom saw that the ring still encircled the bones of Karadin's finger. He lifted the hand, feeling the tingle of energy flowing into him once again – but this time, it was warm and pleasant. It pulsed through his body, soothing his tired muscles, restoring his strength.

The ring is yours! Gargantua hissed.

Tom turned to see the serpent lift her great hooded head. Her eyes shone a bright, dazzling blue, and the deep red reflection of the lava flows swam across her metal scales like flames. Tom saw for the first time that she was beautiful.

Join me, Gargantua said, her voice as soft as velvet. *Put on the ring. You will be strong. You are tired and hurt now, but pain and weariness will be things of the past. You will be the most powerful Master of them all. Together, we can protect this land. No Beast will stand against us.*

In the back of his mind, Tom heard a tiny voice of warning. But he couldn't think why he should not do as the Beast said. With the ring, he could help so many people. He could protect the kingdom and save lives – his whole purpose as Master of the Beasts! With the ring, he and Gargantua could rid Avantia of Evil once and for all.

No! Tom told himself. *I can't take the ring. I can't become like Karadin!* But even as he formed the thought, he was easing the tiny circle of metal off Karadin's bone finger and sliding it on to his own. A tremendous surge of heat flowed through his body as if molten metal ran in his veins. All his pain, all his weakness burned away, until he felt nothing…no weariness, no anger, no fear – just pure, magnificent power.

A TERRIBLE
BETRAYAL

As Tom stumbled from the tunnel
mouth and out into daylight, shading
his eyes, a thin girl with short choppy
hair hurried towards him. She was
smiling as if relieved. Tom stared
at her, trying to place her… Then
suddenly, he remembered. *Elenna!* He
quickly put his hand behind his back,

hiding his new ring.

Clever young Master, Gargantua hissed in his mind. *Don't let anyone see...*

"What happened?" Elenna asked.

"Karadin is dead," Tom said. "Gone for good this time."

Elenna shook her head gravely. "It is for the best," she said. "And the Beast?"

"We don't need to worry about Gargantua either," Tom answered. *Which is true. In a way...*

"Epos has returned to her lair. She isn't back to full strength, but she's much better than she was. Here..." Elenna handed Tom the giant talon of a bird. He found it slotted perfectly into a claw-shaped hole in his shield. "Let's get back to Storm and Silver," she said.

Now that all his aches and pains were gone, Tom found the climb back down the mountain annoyingly slow. Elenna kept stopping to sip from her water flask, and couldn't keep up, no matter how slowly he went.

"Are you all right?" she asked him, staring hard into his face. "You're so quiet. Are you hurt?"

Tom shrugged. He felt a little numb, but compared to all the pain and worry he had been carrying, that was a good thing. "I'm just tired from the Quest," he told her. Still, she didn't stop fussing, insisting he drank some water, asking if he felt sick... By the time they reached the bottom of the mountain, he was fully ready to do what he knew he must. He let Elenna go ahead of him to greet the animals, and softly slid his sword from its sheath. He began tiptoeing towards her...

Elenna spun around as if she had eyes in the back of her head. "Tom?" she said, looking puzzled.

Now! Gargantua hissed. *There can only be one Master of the Beasts. You do not need her. She will only try to steal your glory. You can tell the others she died bravely, fighting Karadin...*

As Tom advanced on the girl, she

snatched the bow from her back and
fitted an arrow to it, taking aim.

"Don't do this!" Elenna said. Her
gaze fell to the ring on his finger.
"Gargantua has enchanted you. You
have to fight her Evil magic!"

Bitterness rose inside Tom. "Fight?
Fighting is all I ever do. I fight
everyone's battles but my own. This

time, I'll fight for what I want. For myself."

"You can't fight for yourself if you aren't yourself," Elenna said. Her arrow was pointed right at Tom's heart, but her eyes were full of some foolish emotion...pity, perhaps.

Tom realised something, and smiled. "You won't shoot me," he said. "You're too weak!"

He lunged and swung his sword for Elenna's chest. She leapt back, so Tom swung again. This time, Elenna darted sideways. But Tom knew that eventually she would grow tired. He just had to wait. He jabbed and slashed, while Elenna danced out of reach or blocked with her bow.

She kept asking him to take off his ring, which made no sense – it was part of him now. *It's just a matter of time...* Tom swung his sword again. Elenna's boot hit a rock as she leapt aside. Her foot skidded from under her and she tumbled. Tom was on her in an instant, ready to finish what he had started.

A sudden, furious snarl stopped Tom in mid-strike. He registered a huge, shaggy grey shape bundling towards him just as pain exploded in his arm. *Elenna's wolf!* The mutt wrenched Tom sideways, his jaws clamped shut on Tom's arm. Elenna struggled to her feet as Silver worried at Tom's limb, gnawing the flesh.

"Get off me!" Tom shouted, lifting his free fist to crush the wolf's skull, ignoring Elenna's angry screams. *Thunk!* Tom felt a sharp stab of pain just above his knee. He looked down to see an arrow sticking out from his leg. Elenna's arrow. A terrible fury rose inside him.

"You shot me!" he cried.

"You left me no choice!" Elenna said. Her face was mottled and there were tears in her eyes. "Tom, you have to take off the ring!" The grey wolf had slunk to Elenna's side and was watching Tom warily. Storm had drawn up alongside them, looking unsettled as he tossed his head and snorted.

Tom felt a sudden lurch of dizziness. His senses swam. For an instant, he felt as if he was locked in a bad dream. He shook his head to clear the feeling.

Kill her... Gargantua hissed.

Tom looked again at the girl. At Elenna. Her eyes pleaded with him. She was trembling. The sight pulled at something deep inside Tom – something that hurt far more than the arrow in his leg. *She's my best friend,* he told Gargantua. *I can't harm her.*

But you must, the Beast replied. *You will...*

Tom could feel his mind going blank again, the strange numbness creeping back...

"Elenna, run!" he cried. "I can't fight Gargantua. She is too strong. I will kill you if you don't go!"

Elenna shook her head. "I won't leave you!" she said. The nagging pain of the arrow in Tom's flesh drew his attention.

You said I would feel no pain, Tom told Gargantua.

You have all the power of four Beasts. Pain is nothing to you now... Kill the girl!

Elenna vaulted up on to Storm's

back. Tom felt a flicker of relief.
She's going to leave…

But then Elenna wheeled the stallion around to face him. Rage boiled up inside Tom. A fury so powerful he knew she would stand no chance against it. The fury of a Beast trapped beneath a mountain for centuries on end. In a desperate attempt to free his mind from Gargantua's control, even for a moment, Tom bent and yanked the arrow from the flesh of his leg. It stung, and blood spurted and gushed from his wound, but he didn't care.

"Go!" he roared at Elenna. "Run, now…or I will kill you!"

6

CONSTRICTED

"I'm sorry, Tom," Elenna said, her eyes filled with regret, then she jabbed her heels into the horse's sides. The animal reared, forelegs wheeling. Tom tried to dodge, but wasn't quick enough... The massive hooves struck him square in the chest, throwing him backwards. Tom's head cracked against the ground, blinding him with agony. Woozy and nauseous, he tried to blink the white spots away from his vision. But he couldn't move – a hot, heavy weight rested on his chest, pinning him to the ground. When his vision finally cleared, he found himself staring into the amber eyes of the wolf, who growled softly, teeth bared.

Craning his neck, Tom saw Elenna slip from the saddle and crouch down at his side. As she took hold of his wrist, panic flared inside him.

Don't let her take it! Gargantua hissed.

Tom tried to snatch his hand from Elenna, but her grip was strong. He

bucked and writhed, but the wolf
flexed its claws, digging them into
his flesh. It was hopeless. Elenna
drew the ring from Tom's
finger…and all
at once his
exhaustion
and pain, his
dread and
worry flooded
back. Every
single part
of him hurt
– especially

his wounded leg. But along with
the pain, a fierce joy spread
through Tom. He was himself once
more. He was free!

"Argh!" Elenna cried, dropping the ring quickly into her pocket, then blowing on her burned fingers. A few tendrils of yellow smoke hung in the air, along with the stink of eggs.

"I'm sorry," Tom said. Silver, still sitting on Tom's chest, stared hard into his eyes for a long moment, then started licking his face. Tom looked up as Storm nuzzled his shoulder, clearly glad to have his master back.

"I thought we'd lost you!" Elenna said, tears streaming down her face. "I know how hard you must have fought against Gargantua's Evil. We have to stop her, once and for all."

Tom nodded. "I have never known a Beast with a more seductive voice. That ring will need to be destroyed, but first—"

BOOM! Chunks of rock and billowing dust filled the air. Silver leapt from Tom's chest with a growl and Tom scrambled up to see Gargantua burst headfirst through a giant hole she had smashed in the mountain. Out in the open, the mighty serpent seemed bigger than ever – a living battering ram the size of a tree. The Beast opened her jaws and let out a furious hiss that turned Tom's guts to water.

"Get behind me," he told Elenna, lifting his sword. With another hiss, the iron snake opened her jaws, revealing deadly iron fangs as long

as Tom's arm that dripped with inky venom.

You are weak! Gargantua hissed in Tom's mind. *Pathetic... unworthy of the title of Master! My ring was wasted on you, and now you shall taste my venom!*

Gargantua darted towards Tom, her cobra's hood fanning open and her mouth gaping wider than ever.

Elenna sent an arrow whizzing through the air, but it pinged harmlessly off the Beast's iron scales. Tom braced himself as the cobra drew close...then, at the last possible moment, he blocked with his shield and stabbed upwards at the same time. He felt a terrific *thud* when the serpent's fangs pierced the wood of his shield and held on as his sword slid harmlessly off the snake's scales. Before he could strike again, Gargantua shook her head, wrenching his shield from his grip.

Tom backed away, desperately looking for a chink in the Beast's armoured flesh. But her iron

hide was sheeny and smooth –
impenetrable.

Elenna fired another arrow.
Again, it skittered off Gargantua's
body. And now the giant serpent
was rising up, her wide flat head
swaying from side to side. Venom
dripped from her fangs, hissing and
smoking where it hit the ground,
and her huge glowing eyes fixed
on Tom.

"Surely she has a weak spot!"
Elenna cried.

"Only the ring," Tom said. "If I put
it on, I can command her. But it's
too big a risk."

Gargantua hissed again, a long,
drawn out sound – like laughter, but

full of hatred.

"Tom, watch out!" Elenna screamed, just as Gargantua's tail lashed and snatched Tom's feet from beneath him. He landed with a painful thump and tried to stand, but Gargantua wrapped herself around him, pulling him back to the ground, and squeezed. Coils of cold, hard metal tightened around Tom's body. He couldn't breathe. With a sickening *crack!* he felt one of his ribs snap, then another.

Tom heard the *twang* of Elenna's bowstring. The *clatter* as her arrow hit the Beast's scales. Storm whinnied and Tom felt the force of his stallion's hooves against

Gargantua's crushing coils. Gratitude welled up inside him. But the snake-Beast only squeezed him harder. Tom felt like his skull would explode with the pressure in his head. His vision blurred and the blue sky above began to fade...

Tom knew that would be the last thing he saw. *She's going to crush me to death!*

7

LAST STAND

Darkness enveloped Tom. *This is it… I've failed Avantia… I'm going to die!*

But suddenly he realised the darkness was real, not just the fading of his sight. Epos hovered above him, blocking out the sun with her colossal wings. And though she still looked weary and hurt,

with her wing feathers bent out of
shape and her golden sheen gone,
she dived towards Gargantua.

The flame bird lashed out, raking
her talons at the snake's iron scales,
sending out sparks and tearing a

gash. Gargantua hissed with rage, and Tom felt the deadly coils that held him loosen. Drawing on his last scrap of strength, he scrambled free to see Epos swipe for the iron serpent again.

Gargantua uncoiled, rising up to meet Epos's attack, her metal fangs snapping at the phoenix. Epos twisted her body to dodge the serpent's bite, then dived again, slicing another deep cut into Gargantua's metal hide.

Tom and Elenna watched in awe as the two Beasts fought. Gargantua was far bigger, and had come to the battle fresh, but Epos showed no fear. She jabbed at the serpent with her sharp beak and slashed with her talons. Gargantua hissed and snapped, each deadly strike faster than the last, but somehow Epos wheeled out of reach.

"I've got an idea!" Elenna said, quickly fitting an arrow to her bow. She aimed it at Gargantua and fired. The arrow slammed straight into a wide gash that Epos had torn in Gargantua's side and lodged there.

"Good plan!" Tom said. But still, the iron serpent didn't slow. She snapped at Epos again and again. While Gargantua fixated on the flame bird, Elenna fired another arrow. Seeing an opening, Tom attacked the Evil Beast from behind. He managed to deepen one of the cuts on the serpent's long, armoured tail. Gargantua must have felt the bite of his blade because her head snapped around. Her eyes flashed with hatred as she lunged for Tom, venom spurting from her fangs.

Tom hunkered down and raised his sword, ready to meet the attack, but with the vast Beast filling his vision, his throat went dry. He knew he was no match for Gargantua. A shadow fell across him from above and, looking up, Tom saw Epos dive towards Gargantua. With a screech of fury, the flame bird sank the talons of both feet deep into the flesh of the serpent's back, clinging on, stopping the snake dead in her path. Instead of striking Tom, Gargantua twisted her head around and sank her iron fangs into Epos's feathered chest.

Epos screeched with pain and frantically flapped her wings, but didn't loosen her grip on the serpent. Elenna seized the opportunity to fire at Gargantua again, her arrow lodging in an open wound. But Gargantua, writhing and lashing her tail, just sank her fangs deeper into Epos.

Tom could feel the Good Beast's anguish. He put his hand to the red jewel in his belt.

Epos! Let go... Flee and save yourself. Elenna and I will finish this fight.

Too late, Epos said, her voice in Tom's thoughts sounding hoarse and strained. *Too late. Gargantua's venom will blacken my heart. I feel its power already. I...have only one choice.*

Flapping her wings with steady, powerful beats, Epos rose slowly into the sky, dragging the immense weight of Gargantua with her. The serpent finally seemed to realise the tables had turned, and opened her jaws, revealing the two deep puncture marks on Epos's chest. The

serpent twisted and hissed,
contorting her body into coils and

knots trying
to get free as
Epos carried
her higher
and higher
into the air.

Tom
suddenly felt
cold. He knew
what Epos
was going to
do. And he
couldn't bear
to watch.

Epos, no! Tom called to the
phoenix.

I must... Epos replied, flapping towards the summit of Stonewin Volcano. *To save Avantia...*

Tom shook his head. His stomach churned with sickening certainty. He had seen Epos rebirth herself in the fires of Stonewin Volcano before. But something about the weariness in her voice, the dullness of her feathers, told him that this time, it would be different.

This time, the phoenix would not rise from the ashes.

Please, don't! he called to Epos.

She had reached the top of the volcano and hovered there for a moment. Gargantua dangled in her grip, wriggling like a worm. The

flame bird, though injured and
dull, was still a magnificent sight
– a brave and beautiful creature of
honour and grace. *I gladly sacrifice
myself for the good of the kingdom*,
she told Tom.

Then she dipped her head and
dived.

Tom sank to his knees, weak
with sorrow as he watched the
phoenix and serpent disappear
into the mountain. *BOOM!* The
ground beneath him quaked, and
a tremendous jet of flames shot up
from the volcano. The flames were a
pure, dazzling gold – so bright, Tom
was momentarily blinded. When
he could see again, the volcano lay

dormant once more, with only wisps of white smoke drifting into the sky. Tom felt a shift in his heart, and glanced at his shield, which lay on the ground not far from him. The phoenix talon embedded in the wood had turned as grey as ash.

Epos the Flame Bird was gone.

HONOURING THE PHOENIX

The following day, Tom and Elenna stood in the cool, dusky torchlight of the Gallery of Tombs with Daltec and Aduro, both dressed in their ceremonial wizard's robes. Tom's leg was bandaged, and his other wounds had also been tended to. But the wound in his heart left by

Epos's sacrifice felt as if it might never heal.

Aduro gestured to the four torches that lined the walls of the crypt,

 only one of which was lit. The old man had tears in his eyes, just as Tom did, and there was a catch in his voice when he spoke. "When a Good Beast dies, it is our custom that a Master or Mistress of the Beasts extinguishes the flame of the

Beast's torch, in their honour. Epos is the last of the fabled four – the ancient Beasts who helped Tanner and the other heroic riders save the kingdom from the villain Derthsin. With her passing, an era of Avantian history comes to an end."

Tom bowed his head, too choked with emotion to reply. He knew that without Epos, he would have perished on this Quest. He thought of how close he had come to succumbing to Karadin's curse himself. Earlier that day, he and Elenna had destroyed the ring in the fires of the palace forge. Gargantua would never rise again.

Elenna touched Tom's sleeve, and

he lifted his head to see the familiar, shimmering form of a spirit standing in front of them – Loris. And at Loris's side was another barrel-chested, bearded ghost whom Tom had only seen before in visions. Mandor – once the King of Avantia, and Loris and Karadin's father. Loris was clearly visible now, and no longer stooped. Though there was still sorrow in the Good spirit's eyes there was pride, too.

"Do not judge my son Karadin too harshly," Mandor said. "There was good in him once, long ago. I am sorry and ashamed for the wrong he has done to Avantia, but I hope now he can rest in peace."

Tom felt too raw from the loss of Epos to answer. A Good Beast had died because of Karadin's crimes. But Tom found he could not hate the ancient prince. After all, Tom had felt the power of the ring, and of Gargantua's voice, for himself. He nodded. "May he rest in peace," Tom managed at last.

Mandor and Loris both smiled and bowed their heads. "Then we too can rest, safe in the knowledge that brave heroes still defend our kingdom," Mandor said. And with that, the two ghosts faded into the shadows, leaving Tom and Elenna to mourn their friend.

Aduro cleared his throat softly.

"Elenna, Daltec, we must leave Tom now to complete his duty as Master of the Beasts."

Tom shook his head. "Don't go!" he said. "I'm not ready." In his heart he wasn't sure if he ever would be.

Elenna put a hand on his shoulder and squeezed. "You can do this," she whispered. Then she, Daltec and Aduro left the chamber.

Tom was alone in the peaceful quiet of the flickering torchlight. He approached Epos's monument – a stone statue of the flame bird with her great wings spread wide. He laid the healing talon at the statue's feet.

"Thank you for your gift," Tom said, just about managing to keep

his voice steady. "So many times, it has meant the difference between success and failure on my Quests – the difference between life and death." Now Tom's voice did waver.

"I can't believe I will never see you again, and never hear your wise voice through my red jewel." Tom put a hand to the ruby in his belt, half hoping to feel even a tingle of warmth. But it was cold. He rested his hand on the cool, smooth stone of the monument. "Sleep well, my friend," he said. "I hope, somewhere, you can hear me. While there is blood in my veins, I will never forget you, and I will ensure your heroic deeds are remembered as long as Avantia stands."

Tom drew a shuddering breath and blinked tears from his eyes. *Can I really do this? Can I say goodbye for ever?* His hand shook as he took up the metal snuffer, but he knew he had no choice. In one quick movement, before his will could falter, he covered the glowing flame, extinguishing Epos's torch. With the chamber now plunged into darkness, Tom turned to leave.

As he was climbing the narrow steps from the crypt, Tom heard a soft *whump!* and a flare of torchlight from behind him cast his shadow on to the stairway wall. His heart beating fast, he turned to see Epos's torch burning brightly again. Stunned, and filled with hope, Tom hurried back to the statue and put his hand on the stone of her chest. It felt warm! Tom grinned, his chest swelling with hopeful joy.

Maybe, just maybe...the flame bird would rise again!

THE END

CONGRATULATIONS, YOU HAVE COMPLETED THIS QUEST!

At the end of each chapter you were awarded a special gold coin.
The QUEST in this book was worth an amazing 8 coins.

Look at the Beast Quest totem picture opposite to see how far you've come in your journey to become

MASTER OF THE BEASTS.

The more books you read, the more coins you will collect!

Do you want your own
Beast Quest Totem?
1. Cut out and collect the coin below
2. Go to the Beast Quest website
3. Download and print out your totem
4. Add your coin to the totem

www.beastquest.co.uk

READ THE BOOKS, COLLECT THE COINS!
EARN COINS FOR EVERY CHAPTER YOU READ!

550+ COINS
MASTER OF THE BEASTS

410 COINS
HERO →

350 COINS
WARRIOR

230 COINS
KNIGHT →

180 COINS
SQUIRE

44 COINS
PAGE →

8 COINS
APPRENTICE

550+
515
480
445
410
395
380
365
350
320
290
260
230
217
206
191
180
146
112
78
44
30
19
8

READ ALL THE BOOKS IN SERIES 27:
THE GHOST OF KARADIN!

GOROG
THE FIERY FIEND

DEVORA
THE DEATH FISH

RAPTEX
THE SKY HUNTER

GARGANTUA
THE SILENT ASSASSIN

Don't miss the first book in this series: GOROG THE FIERY FIEND!

Read on for a sneak peek...

THE BURIED HAND

The clang of steel on steel jerked Tom from his sleep, setting his pulse thudding. He sat up, reaching for his sword. *Is the palace under attack?* But then he heard a cheerful shout from outside, followed by a laugh, and he remembered: the noise was no battle. Captain Harkman's workmen were fixing the palace drainage system. Tom lay back down with a groan, pulling his warm bedclothes tighter, trying to find sleep again, but another loud bang was followed by the rhythmic ringing of a pickaxe on stone.

He sighed. *This is hopeless!*

He rubbed his eyes and swung his legs out of bed. It was barely dawn and thin silvery light filtered through the gap in the shutters. Setting his feet on the chilly flagstones, Tom shrugged his tunic over his head, yanked on his boots then left his room.

I may as well get breakfast!

Elenna was already ahead of him, making her own way down to the kitchens. "Good morning!" Tom called. As his friend turned, he had to stifle a grin. Scowling fiercely and with her short hair sticking up in messy tufts, she looked even grumpier about being up than him.

"Good?" Elenna grumbled. "I don't see what's good about it. How long does it take to fix a few pipes? And I still don't understand why work has to start so early! Every. Single. Day."

Tom chuckled. "After all the places we've slept on our Quests you're bothered by a bit of noise? Although, I have to admit, there's something about being woken at the crack of dawn when you're tucked up in a feather bed that does grate a little." He shrugged. "But the sooner they start, the sooner they'll finish, I suppose."

"Well, it can't be soon enough for me!" Elenna replied, pushing open the door to the kitchens. A warm burst of air engulfed Tom, along with the smell of bacon frying. His stomach growled in anticipation and he felt instantly more cheerful. But before he could enter, a sharp, fearful cry from outside pulled him up short.

"Fire!" another voice yelled from the courtyard.

Elenna turned to Tom with a sigh.

"Sounds like breakfast will have to wait," she said.

Tom nodded. "We'd better find out what's going on!"

They hurried together through the palace and headed out into the chilly dawn to see King Hugo already striding across the courtyard towards the stable block. Brownish smoke coiled upwards from the worksite near the stables where the drainage was being repaired. Tom felt a jolt of worry for the horses and quickened his step.

"Get back!" Harkman cried, urgently shooing three burly workmen away from a jagged trench in the ground. The workmen gaped at the hole, their shovels and pickaxes hanging limply in their hands as more smoke billowed up.

"What's going on?" King Hugo asked, reaching the captain and his men at the same time as Tom and Elenna did.

Harkman gestured to the trench. "In there!" he said. "Some kind of smoke. But there're no flames. And it stinks!"

Elenna clapped a hand over her nose just as Tom got a whiff of the most revolting stench he'd ever smelled. A mix of burned hair, rotten eggs and sewage.

"Move away!" Harkman told his men again. Tom and Elenna stepped

past them to the edge of the trench
and peered down through the smoke,
which spiralled slowly upwards. The
smell was so bad it made Tom's head
swim.

"What's that?" Elenna said,
pointing downwards. Right in the
bottom of the hole, partly covered
by dirt, Tom spotted a rectangular
metal object, about the length of
his forearm,
and covered
in rust. A few
final wisps of
smoke cleared,
and Tom saw it
was some kind
of box.

"Careful," he cried, as Harkman leapt down to retrieve it.

The captain quickly brushed away loose soil and prised the container free. "It's just an old box," he said, climbing back out of the hole and holding the object where everyone could see it. "There are some markings on the top, though." The metalwork was so corroded it was hard to make out the etchings, but, peering closely, Tom saw twin swords, crossed above the hilt.

"That looks almost like a coat of arms," King Hugo said, rubbing at his beard. "But not one I recognise."

Harkman gave the lid a tug. "It's rusted shut," he said.

"What's going on?" Daltec asked, arriving at the worksite with his cloak pulled crookedly over his nightgown. His face creased. 'What's that dreadful smell?'

Harkman held up the box. "It came from the hole where we found this," he said. "But it won't open."

Read
GOROG THE FIERY FIEND
to find out what happens next!

Don't miss the
thrilling new series
from Adam Blade!

FROM THE CREATOR OF **Beast**Quest
ADAM BLADE
SPACE WARS

CURSE OF THE ROBO-DRAGON